This igloo book belongs to:

igloobooks

Published in 2015
by Igloo Books Ltd
Cottage Farm
Sywell
NN6 0BJ
www.igloobooks.com

SHE001 0715
2 4 6 8 10 9 7 5 3 1
ISBN: 978-1-78440-819-0

Illustrated by
Kim Barnes
Mary Bellamy
Lucy Fleming
Sarah Jennings

Additional colour by
Dave Shephard

Stories by
Katie Dale
Jenny Jinks

Printed and manufactured in China

A Treasury of
Bedtime
Stories

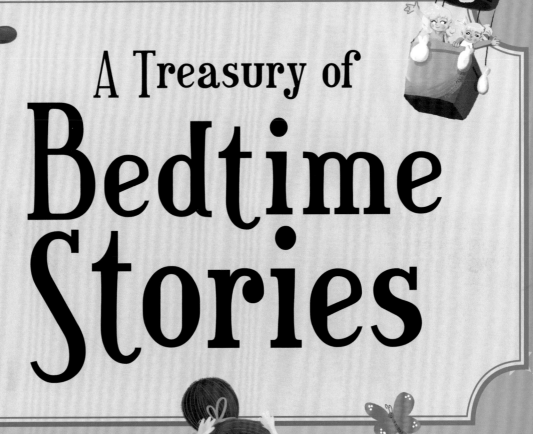

igloobooks

Contents

Nina's New Room

Nina's bedroom was always a mess. She shared it with her younger sister, Millie and there were toys, books and clothes everywhere. They didn't have space for two beds, so Nina and Millie shared bunk-beds. Each night, Nina had to climb over piles of her and her sister's things before she could get into bed. One night, poor Nina had finally had enough of the mess.

"It's not fair," complained Nina to Mum, as Millie played happily below her. "Maybe you have outgrown this room," said Mum, looking around her. "How would you like to have your own room?"
"Really?" asked Nina, excitedly. "I'd love it!" Finally, she would have space for all of her things, without all of Millie's stuff everywhere. Nina couldn't wait and she was so excited, she wanted to get started on her new room straight away.

Nina's New Room

"We'll need to decorate your room first," said Mum. "Why don't we choose some paint together?" So, Mum and Nina went to the paint shop and when they got back, they tried out every shade. Still, Nina couldn't decide.

"I'll paint a rainbow," said Millie. "That will help you to choose!"
"That's a brilliant idea," said Nina, brightly. "We can paint it together."

Nina and Millie had loads of fun slopping paint all over the walls and everywhere else, too! Finally, Nina chose the colours she wanted for her brand new bedroom.

When they'd finished painting, Nina's room looked a complete and utter mess, with paint, boxes and toys everywhere, but Nina didn't mind. It was her very own mess and soon it would all be exactly as she wanted it.

When Nina's room was almost ready, she started to feel nervous. She always complained about how cramped and messy it was sharing a room with Millie, but secretly, Nina loved having her little sister around. Who would she say goodnight to before bedtime now? Who would she play with first thing in the morning? What about if she felt scared after the lights were out?

"Maybe I don't want my own room after all," thought Nina, but then, she had a brilliant idea.

She went all around the house collecting cushions, pillows and her old sleeping bag.

She even found a few of Millie's toys and secretly brought them to her new room. Soon, everything looked perfect.

Nina's New Room

Before she knew it, Nina was ready for her first night in her new bedroom. Then, Millie poked her head around the bedroom door. "Goodnight," said Millie, feeling sad when she saw Nina in her own room without her.

"Not so fast!" said Nina, jumping out of bed and tickling Millie. "I have a surprise for you... Ta-da!" Nina pulled out a mattress from under her bed, with her sleeping bag on it and lots of comfy pillows arranged perfectly. "Who's that for?" asked Millie, feeling very confused indeed.
"You!" squealed Nina. "Now we can have sleepovers whenever we want."

Nina's New Room

So, that night, Nina and Millie had lots of fun playing in the new room. They played board games, told stories and had mugs of creamy, hot chocolate with marshmallows. Nina's bedroom quickly became a complete mess, but she didn't mind one bit. She couldn't wait for their next sleepover.

Prince Henry's Sports Day

Prince Henry loved nothing more than sitting quietly in the castle, reading a book or painting a picture. "Come on, Henry!" his friends would cry, as they ran around outside, playing all sorts of games together. Although Henry thought it looked like lots of fun, he was perfectly happy having fun on his own, as he wasn't very good at sport like his friends were.

One day, the king and queen organized a great, big fair for everyone in the whole kingdom. It was a huge event, with stalls, rides and, most importantly, lots of fun races for everyone to get involved with. It was going to be the best day of the year, for everyone except Prince Henry. The king and queen expected him to do well in all the races. After all, he was the prince, but it was Henry's worst nightmare.

Finish

Prince Henry's Sports Day

"Do I have to take part in the races at the fair?" asked Henry.
"Of course you do," replied the queen. "You'll have lots of fun!"
"Don't worry," said the king, noticing how nervous Henry looked.
"You'll do fine," he said, reassuringly. Henry didn't look convinced,
but little did he know, the king had a special plan to help Henry at the fair.

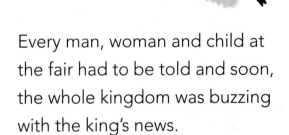

The king had barely finished whispering in his courtier's ear, when the faithful servant sped off to spread his message to the entire kingdom.

Every man, woman and child at the fair had to be told and soon, the whole kingdom was buzzing with the king's news.

Suddenly, there was a loud TOOT-TOOT! as a trumpet sounded to signal the start of the first race.

Henry looked round with dread at his friends at the start of the sack race.
BOING-BOING! he went, as the whistle blew, tripping over with every jump.
He felt certain he would lose, but to his amazement, when he crossed the
finish line, everyone else was in a heap on the grass near the start.
"I've won!" he exclaimed in delight. Maybe the fair wouldn't be so bad.
It wasn't just the sack race, either. Henry kept on winning.

In the egg and spoon race, Henry dropped his egg more times than he could count...

... but somehow, he still came first. Henry couldn't understand it. He thought his friends would beat him in every race.

Then, Henry overheard two girls whispering to one another. "Remember, the king said we must pretend to lose, we don't want to upset the prince." Henry couldn't believe it. Everyone had been pretending all along.

So, in the next race, Henry didn't move. The trouble was, everyone knew they had to let him win, so nobody else moved, either! They all looked at each other, worried, and the crowd looked very confused indeed.

"What should we do?" asked one girl, very quietly. So, Henry turned to face the crowd. "Stop letting me win!" he cried. "I'm not the best at the fair, but it doesn't mean you shouldn't all have fun and try your best."

The king smiled. He realized Henry didn't really need his help after all.

Prince Henry's Sports Day

"Let the games continue!" cried the king and the three-legged race began. Henry stumbled and tripped all the way across the finish line, but when he looked back, he felt disappointed. "You weren't supposed to let me win!" he cried to the others, seeing he'd come first yet again.
"We were the fastest," his partner whispered, sounding every bit as surprised as Henry. The prince clutched his trophy proudly and he couldn't wait for the fair next year.

My Best Friend

My best friend is really special to me.
She's the very best friend there ever could be.
We're always together, never apart.
I hold her close inside my heart.

We love to have tea parties in the sun.
We don't need anyone else to have fun.
Whether we're playing with toys or munching on food,
She always puts me in the happiest mood.

She makes up brilliant games for us to play.
We laugh together every single day.
Whenever we're together, I can't keep a straight face.
I know that she's someone I'll never replace.

My Best Friend

She makes me feel better when I feel all alone.
She really is the best friend I've ever known.
She cheers me up if I'm upset or feel sad.
She makes me see things really aren't so bad.

My Best Friend

Whenever I'm ill, we sit and talk for hours.
She brings me yummy treats, a card and some flowers.
She cheers me up with a joke or a game,
And if she's ever poorly I do exactly the same.

Get
well
soon!

My Best Friend

We always stay out when it's time for bed,
And play out for five more minutes instead.

The thing I love best is that we're always together.
Even better is knowing we'll be friends forever.

The Sleepover

Come in!" said Granny, giving Izzy a big hug and a kiss as she arrived at Granny and Grandad's house. Izzy was having her first ever sleepover without her mum and dad and she felt a bit nervous. "Now, what shall we have for our midnight feast later?" asked Granny. Izzy's eyes lit up. "Midnight feast?" she asked.

"You can't have a sleepover without one," said Granny, smiling.

While Granny was busy in the kitchen, Grandad had a great idea. "Let's make a den!" he said, so they gathered comfy cushions, sheets and blankets from all around the house. They made a tunnel entrance from cardboard boxes and crawled under the table to play, though it was a bit too small for Grandad. "You know what this needs, don't you?" he asked. "Some yummy treats to munch on!"

Izzy and Grandad clunked and clattered around in the kitchen to find a big mixing bowl and a wooden spoon. Izzy squidged and squashed the dough between her hands.

She rolled it around to make delicious chocolate-chip cookie dough. Then, Grandad helped her cut out some funny shapes.

"Let's use purple icing to decorate the cookies," said Izzy, squeezing swirly, gloopy icing on top.

The Sleepover

"Look, Granny!" called Izzy, running into the garden to show her the treats she and Grandad had made. Outside, Granny had set up the picnic table with all of Izzy's paints and lots of paper and brushes.

"Let's do a nice picture for Mummy and Daddy," suggested Granny.

Izzy had great fun slopping her brush in the paint and splattering it all over the paper, making beautiful, swirly patterns and pictures. She couldn't wait to show Mummy and Daddy her paintings.

When Izzy started to get tired, Grandad settled her down for a story before bed, but it was no ordinary bedtime story. "My toys!" cried Izzy, as she saw them all set up on the floor, next to Grandad's special puppet theatre. "Welcome to the show!" cried Grandad, before putting on lots of funny voices for all his puppet characters. Izzy couldn't remember the last time she'd had so much fun and she didn't feel at all nervous any more.

"You haven't forgotten the most important part of a sleepover, have you?" asked Granny, as Izzy climbed into bed after Grandad's toy show.
"The midnight feast!" said Grandad, bringing in a tray filled with all the food Izzy loved the most. They cuddled up on the bed together and munched and crunched on crumbly biscuits and other treats.
"Mmm, delicious," said Izzy, yawning through a mouthful of cupcake.

In the morning, Izzy was woken by lots of clattering downstairs in the kitchen. "Who wants pancakes?" called Granny, up the stairs. Izzy rushed downstairs in her pjs and Granny let her try tossing the pancakes in the pan. They both held firmly onto the handle and FLIP! The pancakes flew through the air. Most of them landed on the floor and Izzy even flipped one so high it stuck to the ceiling. SPLAT! Grandad got a big surprise when one pancake flopped right on top of his head, as Izzy tried to hide her laughter.

Soon, it was time for Izzy to go home. She couldn't believe how quickly
the time had gone. "We've got so much more to do," she said, sadly.
"We have to save something for next time," said Grandad, smiling.
When Mum and Dad arrived, Izzy told them all about the exciting things
she'd done and showed them her lovely paintings.
"It looks like you've had lots of fun," said Mum, smiling kindly. Izzy nodded.
She couldn't wait to have another sleepover at Granny and Grandad's house.

The Great Sheep Chase

Lily, James and Ben loved staying on their grandparents' farm. It was always so much fun helping out. "I like collecting the eggs," said Lily. "Riding on the tractor with Grandad is the best," said James, excitedly. "I can't wait to feed the pigs!" cried Ben, but when they arrived, it was chaos.

"When I opened the gate to the field, all the sheep ran out," said Grandad. The fluffy sheep had scattered all over the farm and were running riot.

"Poor Patch has hurt her paw, too," explained Grandad, "and I can't herd the sheep back into their pen without her." The children smiled at each other.

"Yes you can!" cried Lily, so everyone set to work to round up the sheep.

"Oh, no!" yelled Ben, as one sheep knocked over a bucket of milk. SPLASH!

"Stop it!" called Lily, as another began to nibble on Grandma's special rose bushes. MUNCH!

"Come back!" cried Ben, as two sheep charged straight into a big haystack. Hay flew everywhere, making Grandma sneeze loudly, "ACHOO!"

The sheep managed to disturb some of the other animals, too. Lily found a lamb hiding in the straw in the hen house. "What are you doing here?" she said, picking it up. BAA! went the lamb, nuzzling into Lily's arms. Its wool was soft and warm. "Come on," said Lily. "Let's find your mummy."

The Great Sheep Chase

James found another group of sheep running around the horses' field. "Come on, Grandad!" cried James. "Let's round them up on your tractor." "Great idea, James," said Grandad, as he helped James climb up onto his shiny, red tractor and start the engine. VROOM! The sheep bleated as James and Grandad herded them out of the field and towards their pen.

The Great Sheep Chase

Ben even found a sheep in the pigsty. "Come here!" he cried. BAA, BAA! bleated the sheep, as Ben chased it round the sty, slipping and sliding in the slimy mud. OINK, OINK! squealed the pigs, as they hurried out of the way. "Gotcha!" cried Ben, grabbing the sheep round its tummy, but then WHOOPS! Ben slipped and they both fell into a big puddle of gloopy mud. SPLAT!

Just as Lily and Ben returned the sheep they'd found back to their pen, they heard a yell. "Open the gate!" cried James, as the rest of the sheep came running quickly towards them. Grandad followed close behind in the tractor, trundling through the field. Lily and Ben quickly did as he said and just in the nick of time, too. The sheep raced inside the pen and Grandad locked the gate with a CLICK! Everybody sighed. "Phew!" they said, together.

44

The Great Sheep Chase

"What great teamwork," said Grandad, happily, as they fed the lambs in the barn that evening. "Thank you all so much for your help today," he added.

"You're welcome," smiled Ben, holding the bottle to one lamb's mouth.
"It was so much fun," said Lily, stroking another cute, little lamb's soft wool.
"Can we come back and help tomorrow?" asked James. Grandad smiled.
"You can visit whenever you like," he said. "We love having you here and I can tell you'll all make wonderful farmers when you grow up." The children beamed with delight. They couldn't imagine anything they'd like better.

Al the Alien

Ricky loved space and was forever gazing at the planets and the stars and the moon. He especially loved aliens and wished more than anything that he could meet a real one. One day, Mum and Dad gave Ricky an amazing toy rocket. It had cool, flashing lights and beeping buttons.

"VROOM!" cried Ricky, as he raced it round the room. "I wish it could really take me into outer space for an alien adventure."

That night, Ricky was woken up by a strange sound. BEEP-BEEP! He opened his eyes and blinked, sleepily, then he gasped. "It's my rocket!" he cried in amazement. The rocket door opened and out stepped a tiny, green alien. "Hello," said the alien. "My name is Al. Would you like to go for a ride?"

Al the Alien

Ricky couldn't believe his eyes. There was a real alien in his bedroom!
"You mean," said Ricky, still feeling completely amazed, "you're really from outer space and your rocket can really fly?"
"Of course," said the tiny, little alien. "Hop on-board!" Ricky's face fell.
"I'm much too big to fit," he said. "I can't come with you after all."

Al smiled. He closed his eyes and mumbled something that Ricky thought sounded like gobbledygook. Suddenly, Ricky's arms and legs began to tingle and then ZAP! He found himself sitting inside Al's rocket. "Now you're the perfect size for a ride," cried Al. "Hold on tight!" Al pulled a lever and the rocket blasted off into the air with a great big WHOOSH!

The rocket zoomed out of Ricky's bedroom and down the stairs...

... through the catflap, over the pond and then WHIZZED up into space!

Ricky could hardly believe his eyes, as his house appeared to shrink right below them.

Al the Alien

Up, up, up they went. "This is amazing!" cried Ricky, as they flew straight past the moon. Soon, Ricky and Al were in the middle of outer space, flying and darting among the twinkling stars and magnificent planets.

"Look!" cried Ricky. "There's Venus and Saturn and Mars!" Each planet was even brighter and ten times more beautiful than Ricky had ever dreamed.

Al the Alien

"There's my planet, too," said Al, pointing. "Would you like to visit it?" Ricky nodded, excitedly. He couldn't believe he was going to a real alien planet. The moment they landed, the rocket was surrounded by a group of smiling aliens, each one more wacky-looking than the last. "Hi, Ricky," they said. "Let's have a welcome party to celebrate your visit!"

Al the Alien

Ricky couldn't remember the last time he'd had such amazing fun. He and Al's alien friends played pin-the-tail-on-the-alien, musical rockets and even hide-and-seek, alien style! Then, they had an amazing Purple Planet picnic, packed with the most weird and wonderful treats Ricky had ever tasted. "This is the best party I've ever been to," laughed Ricky.

"I'm glad you've had fun," said Al, with a smile. "We've loved having you to visit, but we'd better be getting back to Earth." The sun was beginning to rise, so Al and Ricky said goodbye to everyone, then climbed into the rocket once more. It was a long way home and, try as he might, Ricky just couldn't stay awake as they zoomed all the way back through space.

The next morning, Ricky opened his eyes and remembered what a fantastic time he'd had with Al on the Purple Planet. To his surprise, he was lying in his bed and was normal size again. Could it all have been a dream? Ricky grinned, as he noticed his toy rocket sitting on the desk. He couldn't wait to find out if Al the alien would take him on another space adventure again.

Princess Daisy's Big Adventure

Princess Daisy loved excitement, but she never got to do anything fun as a princess. She was expected to simply dress up in pretty gowns and learn to sew. She wished she could join in with her brother, Prince Eric, but he wouldn't let her. "You can't play with us," he would reply, when Daisy asked to join in with his friends. "You're a girl!"

One day, Eric was getting ready to set off on his horse, Bramble. Daisy saw Eric and ran up to him. "Where are you going?" she asked. "Can I come?" "I'm going to the orchard to collect apples," he said. "You'd better stay here, princesses can't ride on their own." With that, Eric galloped off into the distance, as Daisy turned around and trudged sadly back to the palace.

Up in her tower, Princess Daisy stared out of the window, daydreaming. She imagined that she was joining in with Eric and his friends, learning to do lots of exciting things, far away from her boring sewing lessons. Suddenly, she heard the CLIP-CLOP, CLIP-CLOP of horse's hooves. "Bramble?" said Daisy, feeling surprised to see her brother's horse.

Daisy ran outside, but she couldn't see Eric anywhere. Bramble had come back all on her own. "Where's Eric?" she asked, as Bramble whinnied. "Let's go and find him!" cried Daisy, jumping on Bramble's back and galloping out of the palace gates on her very own adventure.

Daisy couldn't believe that she was finally having some excitement.
She loved the feeling of the wind through her hair as Bramble galloped
along in the breeze. Finally, Bramble stopped. "Eric?" said Daisy, feeling
puzzled as she saw her brother clinging desperately to a branch, high up in
an apple tree. Eric looked terrified. "Are you alright?" asked Daisy. "I was
so worried when Bramble came back to the palace without you!"

"No I'm not alright!" cried Eric. "I was picking apples when a huge, scary monster went ROAR! and came after me! I had to climb up here to escape." Daisy looked around, but all she could see was a cute, fluffy puppy. "This monster?" asked Daisy, smiling as she looked down at the little puppy. Eric looked very embarrassed indeed. "Let me help you down," said Daisy, smiling kindly. "Then we can go back to the palace."

"Thank you," said Eric, when he was safely back on the ground. "I'm sorry I said you couldn't play with me and my friends. If I let you join in from now on, do you promise not to tell anyone about today?" he asked, nervously. "Don't worry," said Daisy. "Your secret's safe with me. Can I ride Bramble back home?" Eric nodded as he jumped onto Bramble's back with Daisy and they galloped, CLIP-CLOP, all the way home.

Princess Daisy's Big Adventure

From then on, Eric always included Daisy in his adventures and they had fun together every day. He taught her how to do all sorts of exciting things and Daisy never had to have another sewing lesson again. "You're the best brother ever," Daisy would tell him, as they had play-fights in the garden. "You're the most adventurous princess I know," Eric would reply.

Freddie's Party Costume

See you at the party!" called Freddie's friend, George, on the way home from school. "Remember, it's fancy dress." Freddie froze. He'd forgotten all about George's party and didn't have a thing to wear.

"Mum!" cried Freddie, back at home. "I need a costume!"

"Maybe you could make a costume of your own to wear?" suggested Mum.

So, Freddie rushed off to his room. He rummaged all through the dressing-up chest and tipped his craft box upside down. He spent half an hour gluing and sticking, until finally, he was finished. "Okay, ready!" cried Freddie.

"What do you think?" he said, standing proudly in his costume.

"Oh," said Mum, looking in surprise at Freddie's home-made outfit. "What an interesting costume. Maybe we could make something together, though?"

Freddie's Party Costume

Freddie trudged back to his room, after his mum. He searched through his wardrobe while Mum picked up some old boxes from under the bed.
"I suppose I could go as a pirate," said Freddie, pulling on a stripy T-shirt and holding up his longest ruler as a pretend sword. Mum nodded.
"Oh," said Freddie, "but I don't have an eye-patch."

Freddie's Party Costume

Next, Freddie followed his mum into her bedroom while she rummaged around once more. He searched through the chest of drawers, as Mum gathered up some party decorations and a roll of old wrapping paper.

"Maybe I could be a superhero," said Freddie, tying the arms of one of Dad's shirts around his neck as a cape, "but I don't want to have to wear tights like a superhero," he said, looking nervously at a pair of Mum's tights.

Freddie's Party Costume

Freddie headed downstairs to the kitchen, still trudging after Mum. Then he slumped down at the kitchen table. "It's no good!" he wailed.

"Rubbish," said Mum, handing him a pile of odds and ends she'd collected from around the house. Freddie felt really confused.

"Do I have to take the rubbish out?" he asked Mum.

"No, silly!" said Mum, laughing. "This is going to be your costume. All we need is some scissors, glue and paint… and our imaginations, of course!"

Freddie's Party Costume

Mum and Freddie spent all afternoon sloshing paint over the boxes and cutting out shimmery, silvery foil, SNIP, SNIP!

The pile of bits and pieces didn't look very much like anything, but sure enough, as Freddie and Mum worked, slowly, the most incredible costume emerged.

"Hmmm," said Mum, "it still needs a little something..." and she set to work on something extra-special.

Finally, Mum appeared. "Ta-da!" she cried. "This will do the trick."
"Rahhh!" went Freddie. He and Mum had made the best, most fearsome
dragon costume ever. The pretend flames Mum made were the best thing
of all. He gave Mum a huge hug and couldn't wait to show all his friends.

"Wow, you look awesome!" cried George, when Freddie arrived at his party. "Where did you get your costume? You're the best dragon I've ever seen." Freddie grinned and thought about all the fun he'd had with Mum making it. "Oh, it was just lying around at home," he said.

Baby Leo's Bedtime

When Summer's little brother, Leo, was born, everyone was very excited. Everyone except for Summer. Leo didn't do anything fun. He didn't play and he couldn't talk. He just slept... and cried... and burped. "I'm so glad I've got you to play with," said Summer to her teddy, Monty. He was her best teddy and she loved him more than anything in the world.

Then, one night, Leo didn't sleep at all. He cried and cried and cried, "WAA. WAA, WAA!" until everyone was wide awake.

Mummy tried singing while she rocked Leo in the rocking chair.

Daddy tried pulling funny faces and sticking his tongue out.

Granny bounced Leo on her knee, while Grandad piled every toy he could find into the cot.

Summer tried to get to sleep by putting the pillow over her head...

... hiding under the duvet...

... and even putting her fingers in her ears.

Baby Leo's Bedtime

Finally, Summer stopped trying to get back to sleep and thought about baby Leo. "He sounds so upset," she thought, so she got out of bed and padded sleepily down the hall to Leo's nursery. Monty dangled from her hand. "Do you think we can help, Monty?" she wondered out loud.

Baby Leo's Bedtime

"Ssshhh," whispered Summer, "there, there." She leant into Leo's cot and stroked his little, chubby cheeks. "It's alright," she said. Leo looked up at Summer through his teary eyes and all of a sudden, he grabbed Summer's finger with his whole fist. Summer could hardly believe how tiny Leo was.

When she wasn't looking, Monty fell from Summer's hand into the cot. Then, something amazing happened. Leo stopped crying.

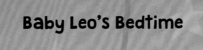

Baby Leo's Bedtime

"What's happened?" asked Mummy, bursting into the room.

"Why has he stopped crying?" yawned Daddy, following in his dressing gown.

"Is the baby alright?" cried Granny and Grandad.

"He's asleep," said Summer, softly. Mum gave a sigh of relief.

"Thank goodness," she said.

Granny and Grandad smiled. "Well done, Summer," they said. "We tried giving Leo all sorts of toys. I wonder why only your teddy bear worked?" "Leo must love Monty because he reminds him of you, Summer," said Daddy, "and he loves his big sister very much." Summer smiled down at her baby brother and suddenly, she felt a lovely, warm feeling inside.

Baby Leo's Bedtime

"Would you mind if Leo borrowed Monty, just for tonight, to help him sleep?" asked Mummy, hopefully. Summer smiled.

"Leo can keep him, she said." Everyone was amazed.

"You love Monty more than anything in the world, don't you?" asked Mummy.

"I have a baby brother now," said Summer, "and it's him I love most of all."

Jenny was going to bed one night.
She kissed and cuddled her mummy tight.
She asked, "does everyone have a lovely home like me?"
Mummy said, "I'll tell you a rhyme and then you'll see."

"Some homes are big and some are small.
Some are flat and some are tall.
Some are round and some are square.
Some you'd hardly know are there."

What Makes a Home

"Some are modern, some are old.

Some are steamy, some are cold.

Some huddle close, some stand alone.

They're made of ice, or wood, or stone."

"Some homes perch on mountains high,
With roofs that almost touch the sky.
Others stand beside a lake.
Some look like they're made of cake!"

"Some homes have a shining light,
Flashing warnings in the night.
Some have turrets, some have towers,
Some have balconies of flowers.

Some homes travel all around,
Up in the air or on the ground.
Some homes sail the seven seas,
Others perch among the trees."

"A home can be made anywhere.

On land, on sea, or in the air.

Whether on the ground, or high above,

What makes a home is lots of love."

"And so, my darling, now you see,
Wherever we may dream to be,
We'll be as happy as can be.
For I've got you and you've got me."

Bella's Ballet Shoes

Bella loved ballet more than anything in the world and she would dance around the house whenever she could. She was always whirling and twirling, leaping and prancing, any chance she got. Bella loved dancing so much that when her cousins came to stay, with their new puppy, she was putting on a special show for them and all her family and friends in the living room. She was so excited that she'd been practising extra-hard.

DING-DONG! WOOF! WOOF! "They're here!" called Bella's mum.
Bella's cousins, Cara and Fiona, ran in, followed by their very bouncy puppy.

"Down, Scruff!" cried Bella, laughing, as Scruff jumped up at her, licking
her all over. The dog obediently sat at her feet. "Good boy," said Bella
patting him on the head. Then, Scruff got excited again and started
licking her pretty ballet slippers. "Hey, that tickles!" she laughed.

Bella's Ballet Shoes

"I know," said Fiona, "let's play with Scruff in the garden." Bella wasn't sure. "I really ought to be practising for my big performance," she thought, but she wanted to play with her cousins, too. So, she changed out of her ballet clothes and followed Fiona, Cara and Scruff into the garden. They had fun throwing sticks and balls for Scruff, then Bella's mum called them inside for lunch. As soon as they'd finished, Bella rushed off to rehearse.

Bella's Ballet Shoes

"Mum!" called Bella, "I can't find my ballet shoes anywhere," she said, looking under the bed.

"They must be around here somewhere," said Mum. So Fiona and Cara looked in the living room, behind all the cushions...

... and Mum looked in all the cupboards, but no-one could find Bella's shoes anywhere.

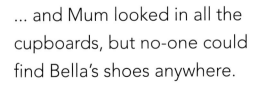

Bella's Ballet Shoes

"They've disappeared!" cried Bella. Then, she looked out of the window. "Scruff, no!" she cried. The naughty puppy was digging in the garden and Bella could just see something poking out of the ground.

Mum, Bella and her cousins all rushed outside and sure enough, there in the flower bed, were Bella's beautiful purple ballet shoes. "They're ruined!" cried Bella, tearfully. "I can't perform now," said Bella, feeling heartbroken. "I'm sorry, sweetheart," said Mum, giving her a hug. "You can still dance without your shoes, can't you?"

Bella's Ballet Shoes

Bella turned and ran upstairs to her room. "It's not the same," she called, feeling really disappointed. She flopped down on the floor, but just then, her cousins knocked on the door. "We've got something for you," said Cara. "It was supposed to be a special present," said Fiona. "We were going to give it to you after your show, but we think you'd better have it now, instead!"

Bella opened the box and gasped. Inside was the most beautiful pair of pink ballet shoes she'd ever seen! "Thank you, thank you!" chattered Bella, slipping the shoes on straight away and getting ready for the show. Everyone else settled down in the living room, eager to see Bella dance.

Bella's Ballet Shoes

When the show started, Bella twirled and danced more beautifully than ever, leaping and gliding elegantly. Everyone clapped and cheered. Even Scruff jumped and barked excitedly! Bella beamed. She felt just like a ballerina in a real show and now she had the best ballet shoes ever, as well.

Poppy's Perfect Playtime

Poppy couldn't wait for her best friend, Holly, to come round and play. She had lots of games planned and Mummy had even made them a picnic to eat together, out in the sunshine. "It's going to be perfect," thought Poppy to herself, just as the doorbell went DING DONG!

When Poppy opened the door, Holly was standing there in her raincoat and rubber boots. "Oh no!" cried Poppy, as the raindrops went DRIP-DROP, PLIP-PLOP, in puddles on the ground. "Now we can't do any of the fun things I wanted to," said Poppy, feeling very disappointed indeed. "Yes we can," said Holly, stepping inside and taking Poppy's hand.

Holly ran into the living room, as Poppy followed closely behind. "Come on, let's play hide-and-seek!" cried Holly. So, Poppy slowly counted to ten. "Coming, ready or not!" shouted Poppy. She searched everywhere she could think of. Behind the door, in the cupboard and even under the sofa.

Suddenly, the curtains moved. "Boo! Found you!" cried Poppy, laughing. "Your turn!" cried Holly, as Poppy dashed off to find the perfect hiding place.

Poppy's Perfect Playtime

When they'd finished playing hide-and-seek, Holly had another
great idea. "Why don't we make a den?" she suggested. Poppy smiled.
She knew exactly what they needed to build their very own cosy den.

Poppy and Holly took the cushions off the sofas and Mummy found them
an extra-large blanket to cover the table with. Then, they dived under the
table and into their soft, pillowy den and played with all of Poppy's best dolls.

Poppy's Perfect Playtime

"What shall we do now?" asked Holly, poking her head out from the den and looking through the window at the rain outside.

"We can't have Mummy's picnic outside," said Poppy. "So why don't we have an indoor tea party, instead?" Poppy and Holly gathered up all of Poppy's teddies and arranged them in a circle in her bedroom.

"SLURP, SLURP!" said Poppy, holding a cup up to her teddy's mouth.

"Here, Mr Bear," said Holly, pouring another cup of pretend tea.

Just then, Mummy knocked on the door, carrying a tray of delicious food. "You can't have a tea party without some teatime treats," she said, "even if it is still raining outside!"

The girls both jumped up, eager to tuck into some of the yummy sandwiches and fairy cakes Poppy had helped her mum make that morning. "This is the best picnic ever," said Holly, taking a bite out of a gooey, squidgy fairy cake.

Just as Poppy and Holly had polished off the last bite of their picnic, Poppy looked out of the window. "Look!" she cried. "It's stopped raining!" The sun was shining brightly and there was a beautiful rainbow in the sky.
"It looks like we can go out and play after all," said Holly.

So, Poppy and Holly pulled on their rubber boots and raced outside to jump in the splashy puddles. SPLISH! SPLOSH! SPLASH! "This is the best day ever!" said Holly, laughing. Poppy smiled. The rain hadn't spoiled their day at all. In fact, it had been absolutely perfect, just the way it was.

Timmy's Travelling Bed

When Timmy went to stay at his uncle's house, he didn't want to go to sleep at bedtime. He was having far too much fun! Then, his uncle told him a special secret he could hardly believe... Timmy's bed was magical!

"All you have to do is snuggle up tight, close your eyes and count to twenty," said Timmy's uncle, "all while thinking of the place you'd like to go. The bed will take you there for a wonderful adventure!"

So, Timmy did exactly as his uncle said. He snuggled up with his toy elephant, closed his eyes tightly and thought of the place he most wanted to go in the whole wide world. Then, slowly, he began to count to twenty...

Timmy's Travelling Bed

Suddenly, Timmy opened his eyes and gasped. "It worked!" he cried. He was in the middle of an amazing safari park. "My bed really is magic," said Timmy.

Just then, a group of cheeky monkeys swung through the trees and grabbed him by the hands. "WHEEE!" he cried, as they soared through the branches.

Timmy had never had so much fun before. The monkeys did great big loop-the-loops with him, before dropping him into the penguins' pool. SPLASH! "Hello, penguins," said Timmy, as the penguins swam and dived in the water. Timmy even joined in to play catch with the penguins and they splashed around happily as he threw the ball back and forth with them.

Next, Timmy found himself being scooped up from the penguin pool. He was put down on the ground by an enormous elephant. PLONK! Then, there was a loud GUSH! as she dried off Timmy with her great big trunk. "Thank you, Mrs Elephant!" called Timmy, through the gust of air.

Timmy's Travelling Bed

Suddenly, Timmy felt a tickle under his arm and giggled. It was an adorable baby elephant, tickling him with her trunk. She looked just like Timmy's very own toy elephant!

Next, Timmy and the baby elephant played chase and had a wonderful time playing together.

Whenever Timmy caught up with her, she squirted him with water. SPLASH!

Timmy's Travelling Bed

Then, the first elephant lifted Timmy onto her back. "Where are we going?" asked Timmy. TRUMPET! she went, as she took him for a ride through the plains in the evening sunshine. Timmy was so high up, he could see the meerkats, zebras and all the other animals. Timmy gazed at everything in wonder, as he rocked from side to side on the elephant's back.

Very soon, he began to feel really sleepy…

Timmy's Travelling Bed

… "Wakey-wakey, Timmy!" his uncle called in the morning. Timmy opened his eyes and found he was back in bed, with his best toy elephant tucked safely under his arm.

"Well?" asked his uncle, smiling as he brought Timmy breakfast in bed.
"Did you have any exciting dreams last night?"
"It was the best night ever," said Timmy. "I can't wait to go to bed tonight!"

Kitty and Katie

Katie's best friend in the world was her cat, Kitty.
She was fluffy and gentle and ever so pretty.
Each day after school, little Kitty would wait,
On the moss-covered wall beside Katie's school gate.
They'd both race back home, just as fast as they could.
How Kitty always won, Katie never understood.

Kitty and Katie

They spent all their afternoons playing together,
They always had fun, whatever the weather.
They'd hunt in the garden and play hide-and-seek.
What Kitty liked best was chasing her toy that went SQUEAK!

Kitty and Katie

The time Katie loved was when day turned to night,
When she could cuddle her Kitty and squeeze her so tight.
Katie would stroke Kitty's soft, fluffy fur,
Then they'd both fall asleep to the sound of her purr.

Kitty and Katie

Then, one day Kitty did not win their race.
She wouldn't play hide-and-seek, hunting, or chase.
The next day when Katie passed by the school wall,
She looked for her cat and there was no sign at all.

116

Kitty and Katie

Poor Katie ran home, looking out for her cat.
She found Kitty fast asleep on her mat.
"Oh, poor little cat," said Katie. "What's the matter?"
"She's just getting old," said her mum, "and a bit fatter!"

Kitty and Katie

Still, Katie knew something just wasn't quite right.
She hugged Kitty close as they curled up that night.
Then, the next morning, Kitty couldn't be found.
Katie searched everywhere, then heard a sound.

Kitty and Katie

"Kitty!" she cried, looking under her bed,
But to her surprise she found kittens, instead.
Katie was so glad that her cat was okay,
And thrilled that she'd brought six new kittens to play.

Dancing Daniel

Daniel loved to dance whenever he could. He just couldn't help himself. He danced any time and all the time.

As soon as he heard any kind of music, he just couldn't keep still. He loved leaping and twisting in the air and making up his own routines to all the best songs.

There was just one problem. Daniel was far too shy to dance in front of other people.

One day, Mum had a surprise for Daniel. "I've signed you up for the new dance club at school," she said. "Isn't that exciting?" Daniel didn't feel very excited at all. He was terrified of everyone seeing him dance. "I've never danced properly before," he thought to himself, remembering all of his made-up routines. "What if I'm not any good?"

Dancing Daniel

On the first day of dance club, Daniel felt really nervous. He liked the idea of learning some cool, new dances, but he was horrified to see how many people were in his class. Surely they'd all be watching him!

So, Daniel made sure he was at the back where no one could see him, then, it was time for the class to begin. "One, two, three!" called the teacher, as everyone followed her dance moves.

Dancing Daniel

At first, Daniel was so scared, he could barely move, but he soon realized that nobody was watching him at all. They were all far too busy concentrating on their own moves, so Daniel slowly started to relax.

"Left, right... one, two, three," whispered Daniel, under his breath, moving his feet to the beat and spinning WHOOSH! in a circle, before punching his arms in the air.

Dancing Daniel

By the end of class, Daniel had tried every kind of dance, from ballroom to break-dancing. He'd skidded across the floor on his knees...

... and whirled around the floor with his partner. He'd danced to fast music and slow music and everything in between.

Then, the teacher made an announcement. "There's a performance next week," she said, "and Daniel will be doing a solo!"

Daniel froze. "I can't perform in front of everyone," he thought, feeling more terrified than ever. When Mum picked him up, the teacher explained how well he'd danced in class and told her all about his solo in the show. "I can't wait to see you dance on stage," said Mum, giving Daniel a hug.

Dancing Daniel

Daniel practised harder than ever for the performance. He still felt scared, but he loved rehearsing all the cool, new moves he'd learnt. TAP, TAP went his feet, lightly across the floor and SNAP, SNAP went his fingers, as he clicked in time to the music. Still, when he thought about going up on stage, it felt like he had butterflies in his tummy.

"Mum, I'm nervous," said Daniel, on the way to the show. "I can't do it."

"Don't worry," said Mum. "It's normal to feel a bit scared."

When he got there, Daniel saw everyone in their costumes. The girls had swirly skirts, the boys wore sparkling tops and best of all, everyone had glittery masks to wear. Daniel felt much better. No one would recognize him if he was wearing a mask during the performance.

As the show was about to start, Daniel took a deep breath and walked on stage. The music started and suddenly, he forgot about all the faces in the crowd. Daniel danced bigger and better than ever before, spinning and jumping perfectly in time to the music. He was having so much fun, that right at the end he pulled his mask off and the crowd went wild.

Dancing Daniel

Everyone came up to Daniel at the end of the show to congratulate him.
"You were amazing," said Mum, proudly.
"We didn't know you could dance like that!" added his friends. Daniel felt very pleased indeed. From then on, he was never too shy to dance in front of other people. In fact, they couldn't get him to stop!

Beth's Birthday Surprise

It was Beth's mummy's birthday, and Beth was planning a very special day for her. While Mummy was out, first Beth and Daddy decorated the whole house with balloons and bunting. Beth loved helping to blow up the balloons, but she always let go of them before she could tie them up, so they whizzed off around the room. WHEEEEEEEEE! Bouncer, their new puppy, barked and chased the whizzing balloons, making Beth giggle.

Then, it was time to make the cake. Beth loved cooking with Daddy, because he made even more mess than she did! Beth loved cracking the eggs the best. She tapped the shells CRACK! and then they dropped PLOP! into the bowl. They mixed everything together. WHIZZZZZZZZZZZ!

Next, they spooned the batter into the tins. "Oh no, we've made too much," said Beth, looking at all the cake batter left in the mixing bowl. "Let's make some delicious cupcakes with the leftover batter," suggested Daddy, finding some cupcake cases in the baking cupboard.

Beth's Birthday Surprise

While they waited for the cakes to cook, Beth decided to make a special, home-made birthday card for Mummy. She painted beautiful flowers and hearts on the front and sprinkled sequins and glitter all over it. Just then, Bouncer bounded outside and knocked over the paint pots, spilling paint all over the grass. Even worse, he walked painty footprints all over Beth's lovely card for Mummy. "Oh no, Bouncer!" cried Beth, feeling disappointed.

When the cake had cooked and cooled down, Beth and Daddy smothered sticky jam in the middle and gloopy icing over it.

Very carefully, they piped beautiful swirls all around the whole cake.

Then, they made little, pink sugar roses to go on top. Beth even got to lick the bowl!

Beth's Birthday Surprise

It was the most delicious cake Beth had ever seen and she couldn't wait to show Mummy. Just then, she heard Mummy's footsteps coming up the path. Daddy quickly picked up their magnificent cake to carry it into the living room, but just then Bouncer came bounding into the hall. Daddy tripped and fell, as Beth watched in horror. The cake went flying and splattered all over the floor. "Oh, no! Bouncer!" cried Beth as the naughty puppy quickly gobbled up Mummy's delicious cake, barking and looking very pleased.

Beth's Birthday Surprise

Beth felt very sad indeed. Their special birthday cake had looked so beautiful and Mummy hadn't even got to see it. Her wonderful surprise was ruined. What were they going to do now? Suddenly, Beth had a brilliant idea.

"Distract Mummy," she told Daddy. "I've got a plan." Beth found the extra cupcakes they'd made and stacked them in a pyramid. She carefully placed lots of delicious sweets and fruit on the cupcake pyramid, sticking them on the gloopy icing on top. It wasn't exactly what she'd planned, but she was sure Mummy would love it just the same.

Suddenly, Beth saw the bouquet of flowers they'd picked for Mummy. One of the flowers had fallen off, so she put it on the very top of the cupcake tower. Then, the door opened and Daddy brought Mummy in to see all her gifts. Beth quickly stood in front of the cakes so her mum wouldn't see. "Happy birthday, Mummy!" cried Beth, giving her a great, big birthday hug.

"Thank you, sweetheart," said Mummy, then she gasped. "Look at that beautiful card, with Bouncer's lovely footprints, too. The cakes look delicious!" Beth couldn't believe it. Her surprises had turned out to be a disaster, but Mummy loved them anyway. "You really like it?" she asked.

"Absolutely," said Mummy, smiling. "This is the best birthday surprise ever."

Super Sam

Sam loved pretending to be a superhero and he wore a pretend superhero cape wherever he went. He could make even the most boring chores seem like an exciting, superhero adventure. "Zap that dirt!" he cried, as he splashed his hands into the sink to do the washing up.

Even cleaning his room was an exciting mission for Super Sam. "Whoosh!" he cried, as he picked up his dirty clothes. Super Sam had a superhero sidekick, too. He loved playing superheroes with his best friend, Mike. "BAM!" they cried, zapping weeds in the bushes. "Mega-alert!" cried Mike, pointing to the neighbour's cat up a tree. "Super Sam to the rescue!" cried Sam, zooming over and bouncing on the trampoline to reach the cat, just as it jumped down from the branches.

One day, Super Sam saw Mrs Green struggling with her bags when he was out with Mum. ZOOOOM! He ran over to help her pick up her shopping. Then, he spotted a poster she'd dropped. "That's my kitten, Shadow," said Mrs Green, sadly. "She's gone missing. She'll be getting hungry and it will soon be dark, too," she said. "I'm terribly worried about her."
"Never fear, Super Sam's here!" cried Sam. "I'll find her for you."

Sam and Mum searched high and low for Shadow. "There she is!" he shouted, pointing in a shop window, but it was just a toy cat.

"Found her!" he cried, racing after a lady carrying something small and black, but it was just her little dog.

"A-HA!," said Super Sam, grabbing a man's black, fluffy hat by mistake. Sam sighed and felt disappointed. He thought maybe he wasn't so super after all.

Super Sam

As they walked home through the park, Sam saw a ball flying through the air.

"Watch out!" he called to Mum, pushing the ball away from her just in time.

"My ball!" cried the little girl, as it rolled into the bushes.

"Super Sam to the rescue," said Sam, as he whizzed off to find the ball.

Then, Sam's super-hearing picked up a faint sound from the bushes.

He bent down, only to spot two little eyes glowing in the darkness, with his super-sight. "Don't worry, Shadow," he said. "Super Sam will rescue you!"

Sam reached into the bush and heard a RIP! as his cape tore on the brambles, but he knew that saving Shadow was more important.

He wrapped his cape around Shadow and she meowed, happily. "That's another successful mission for Super Sam!" he said.

Super Sam

Mrs Green was delighted when Super Sam arrived on her doorstep. "Thank you so much for finding her," she said, stroking the little kitten. "Come in and have some cake," and she led them inside.

As Sam munched away, he watched the kitten playing happily with his superhero cape. "I'm sorry about the rip in your cape," said Mrs Green. "That's okay," said Sam, smiling. "Shadow likes it, so she can keep it now."

The next day, Super Sam heard a DING-DONG at the door. "Sam!" called
Mum. "There's a special present here for you." Sam raced to the door.
Mum handed him a large parcel. Attached to it was a note from Mrs Green.
"Every hero needs a cape," read Sam. He tore open the package to find
a beautiful cape with an 'S' stitched on. "Wow," he said, putting the cape
on and spinning around. "Now I'm a real superhero!"

The Treasure Trail

"Oo-arrr!" cried James. He was all dressed up in his pirate outfit. "I can't wait for Tim to get here," he said. "We'll have so much fun playing pirates together." In the hallway, Mum had just got off the phone.

"Oh dear," she said. "Tim's not very well, I'm afraid he's not going to be able to come and play pirates with you this afternoon."

"Who will I play with now?" wailed James, trudging upstairs. James flopped down on the bed. It was no fun playing pirates alone. Suddenly, he heard a loud noise downstairs. CRASSSHHHHHH! "What could that be?" he thought.

James grabbed his toy sword and went downstairs to investigate. "AHARRRRRR!" he cried, jumping into the living room, swishing his sword, but there was no one there. Then, James realized he hadn't seen Dad anywhere all morning. "Where could he be?" thought James. Just then, there was a great big BANG! James was sure the noise had come from the kitchen. He rushed to look, but yet again, no one was there.

"What's going on?" thought James, sloping off upstairs again. There, to his surprise, on his bed was a real treasure chest! Slowly, James opened it up and inside, he found a real pirate scroll. James quickly unrolled it. Written on the scroll was a message in funny, swirly, pirate writing. "Is there pirate treasure to find?" read James. "Follow the clues I've left behind. The first is hidden below the deck, look under the seats and check."

The Treasure Trail

"That must mean the next clue is downstairs," thought James, but what did 'under your seat' mean? "Of course!" he cried, "Under the sofa cushions!" James raced downstairs to the living room, pulled all the cushions off the sofa and sure enough, there he found another pirate scroll.

The Treasure Trail

"Look behind your most-loved snack," read James, "to find the next message and stay on track." James loved sausage rolls, almost as much as he loved pirates! That had to be what the clue meant.

So, James looked in the kitchen and soon found a bottle of juice with another scroll tied to it. The bottle was labelled 'Pirate Grog, drink me'. "On water sails the pirate ship," read James. "Be careful, or you'll take a dip."

The Treasure Trail

As James drank the delicious Pirate Grog, he heard another BANG! outside, but he was too busy working out the next clue to look. 'Taking a dip?' They didn't have a pool, or a pond. Then suddenly, he had an idea. James ran to the bathroom and sure enough, his toy boat was floating in the bath. There, in the boat, was another scroll. "With your telescope, look through the glass," read James. "You'll find the treasure upon the grass."

The Treasure Trail

James was so excited. The treasure hunt had been so much fun, he couldn't wait to see what was at the end of it. James grabbed his telescope and peered through it. When he did, he couldn't believe his eyes. There, in the middle of the lawn, was a huge, wooden pirate ship!

"Surprise!" called Dad. "Ready for a swashbuckling good time?"

"Aye-aye, Captain," said James, laughing and running down the garden path.

"Come aboard, me hearty," said Dad, "or I'll make ye walk the plank!"

The Treasure Trail

James had great fun playing pirates all afternoon with his dad. They practised walking the plank and his dad even taught him to play-fight with his sword, just like a real pirate. "Who wants some treasure?" asked Mum, carrying out a tray piled high with gleaming golden coins.

"Aha, pirate's gold!" cried James, seeing Mum's treasure.

"Even better than that," said Dad, unwrapping a coin. "Chocolate gold!"

James laughed. It had been the best pirate day ever!

Clumsy Prince Christopher

Christopher was a clumsy prince, who caused chaos wherever he went. On the day of his birthday party, the queen was sure there would be mayhem, but Christopher couldn't wait for his friends to arrive and celebrate with him. He rushed around the palace putting up balloons, accidentally bursting most of them as he went. POP! Suddenly, the palace doorbell went DING-DONG, just as Christopher picked up two plates of wibbly-wobbly jelly. "They're here!" he cried. "Will you hold the jelly for me, Edmund?" asked Christopher, passing the jelly to the palace butler.

Christopher flung the doors open. "Come in!" he cried. As he did, he knocked over his poor butler with his wild, waving arms. "Woooaaahh!" cried Edmund, losing his balance. The jelly flew out of his hands, up into the air and landed all over him with a SPLAT! "Not again," said Edmund, chuckling.

"Follow me," said Prince Christopher to his royal guests, as he marched off into the living room. "Who wants to play a game?" he asked. As he hurried away to get the party started, he slipped on the hall rug and slid headfirst into the kitchen, WHOOSH! Christopher collided with all the pots and pans, CRASH! CLATTER! BANG! "Terribly sorry," called Christopher from the kitchen, as all his friends burst out laughing.

Clumsy Prince Christopher

"Let's play hide-and-seek," said Christopher. He rushed around looking for his friends, but he fell flat on the floor, next to Steven who was hiding under the table. "Found you!"

Next, Christopher stumbled backwards into the curtains, pulling one down on top of himself, revealing two more of his friends hiding behind it.

"Oh, Christopher!" his friends cried, laughing. Parties at the palace were never dull with clumsy Christopher around.

"Let's play musical chairs," suggested Christopher. "Hooray!" cried his friends, as they danced around happily to the music.

As soon as the music stopped, everyone dashed to find a chair to sit on. Christopher rushed to get the last chair at the same time as Simon and...

... BUMP! They crashed into one another and landed in a heap on the floor. Everyone laughed so hard they fell off their chairs, too!

Clumsy Prince Christopher

Next, it was time for a game of pin-the-tail-on-the-donkey. Christopher put on the blindfold and stumbled clumsily across the room. "Where's the donkey?" he asked, waving his arms around wildly, accidentally knocking over a vase. As Edmund bent down to pick it up, Christopher stuck the tail on Edmund's bottom! "Ooops!" said Christopher. He and his friends roared with laughter, with Edmund laughing louder than everyone.

At last, it was time for Christopher's birthday tea. The queen brought out a huge birthday cake, fit for a prince. Christopher couldn't wait to taste it, but as he stepped towards the cake, he tripped and fell. "WHOOOAAAA!" he cried, as he fell straight into the middle of the cake, head first. He was covered in gloopy icing and he licked his lips. "Mmmm, delicious," he said.

Everyone roared with laughter. "Never mind," said the queen. "It's a good job Cook's made a spare cake, just in case something like this happened!" "This is the best party ever," said Christopher, still covered in sticky icing. All his friends agreed. They'd had such a great time at the party and Christopher was so funny, they couldn't wait to come back and play again.

The Wishing Star

When the day turns into night and all the stars are shining bright,
Try to see if you can spy the brightest star up in the sky.
That's the wishing star, my dear. So when you see that star appear,
You must close your eyes up tight and make a wish with all your might.

The Wishing Star

You can wish for anything...

... to be a princess, prince or a king.

To sail a boat or drive a train, or even fly high in a plane.

The Wishing Star

You can wish to go to any place...

... the jungle, desert, or outer-space!

Climb a mountain, topped with snow...

... or trek through deep, dark caves below.

You can wish to be a diver,

or a high-speed racing driver.

You can wish to be a farmer,

or be a knight in shining armour.

You can wish to be a great inventor,

or a kids' TV presenter.

You can be a great magician,

a painter...

... or musician.

The Wishing Star

You can wish to have a band and play your songs throughout the land.
You can wish to dance, or act, or sing. You can wish for anything!

The Wishing Star

So make your wish, curl up tight and have sweet dreams all through the night.
What you wish is up to you. For one day, it might just come true.

The Troublesome Twins

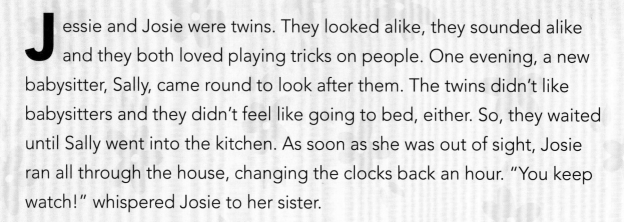

Jessie and Josie were twins. They looked alike, they sounded alike and they both loved playing tricks on people. One evening, a new babysitter, Sally, came round to look after them. The twins didn't like babysitters and they didn't feel like going to bed, either. So, they waited until Sally went into the kitchen. As soon as she was out of sight, Josie ran all through the house, changing the clocks back an hour. "You keep watch!" whispered Josie to her sister.

The twins ran upstairs, expecting to have a whole extra hour to play before bedtime, but a few minutes later, Sally called to them up the stairs. "Bedtime, girls!" cried Sally.
"It's not 7 o'clock yet," grumbled Jessie, but to her surprise, all the clocks they had changed were pointing to 7 again. The twins felt confused. Why hadn't their clever trick worked?

"Come on," said Jessie, grinning at her sister. "We can still play a trick on Sally before bed." So, the twins rummaged in their big box of special tricks and pulled out an enormous, fake, hairy spider! "Let's see what happens when we leave this at the top of the stairs," said Jessie.

The Troublesome Twins

The twins rushed into the bathroom to brush their teeth and waited for Sally's terrified scream, but instead, Sally simply walked in, smiling. "Are those teeth sparkly white, yet?" she asked, brightly. Jessie and Josie couldn't believe it. "How could she not have seen the spider?" whispered Jessie to Josie.

The twins felt disappointed, but knew they had one more trick up their sleeve.
Jessie got ready for bed, then there was a loud scream. "AHHHHHHHHH!"
There, in the middle of her bed, was their missing fake spider. At the same
time, Josie pulled back her own duvet and BOING! A real, live, slimy green
frog jumped out at her. She screamed even louder than Jessie, then turned
and frowned, only to see Josie frowning right back at her.

The Troublesome Twins

"You tricked me!" they both cried, pointing at one another. Just then,
Jessie and Josie both turned to see Sally, trying to hide her laughter.
"It was you?" asked Jessie, surprised. Sally smiled and nodded.
"How did you know about our tricks?" asked Josie, laughing.
"I loved playing tricks when I was your age," said Sally, with a twinkle
in her eye, "especially on my babysitters!"

Jessie and Josie spent the rest of the evening hearing all about Sally's tricks. She had a special flower that squirted water at people and she showed them how to stuff socks into shoes so they wouldn't fit. She even poked a jelly worm through an apple. It looked so disgusting! Jessie yawned and plonked down on a cushion. "Come and sit with us," she said to Sally. BBBRRRPPPP! The twins fell about laughing, as Sally pulled their whoopee cushion from under her. "It looks like we managed to trick you after all," said Josie.